LOVABLE FURRY OLD GROVER'S
RESTING PLACES

A Random House PICTUREBACK®

 Published in the United States by Random House, Inc., New York, and simultaneously in Canada by Random House of Canada Limited, Toronto, in conjunction with the Children's Television Workshop. *Library of Congress Cataloging in Publication Data:* Stone, Jon. Lovable furry old Grover's resting places. (A Random House Pictureback) "Book was created in cooperation with the Children's Television Workshop"—SUMMARY: Grover demonstrates the special resting places he has for every part of his body. [1. Puppets—Fiction] I. Henson, Jim. II. Smollin, Michael, ill. III. Children's Television Workshop. IV. Sesame Street (Television program) V. Title. PZ7.S87785Ad 1984 [E] 83-21087 ISBN: 0-394-86056-X Manufactured in the United States of America 7 8 9 0

LOVABLE FURRY OLD GROVER'S RESTING PLACES

written by JON STONE
illustrated by MICHAEL J. SMOLLIN

Featuring Grover,
a Jim Henson
Sesame Street Muppet

Random House / Children's Television Workshop

This is a
RESTING PLACE.
Let me show
you how it works.

TOLLY

It is an
ELBOW
RESTING
PLACE!
SEE?

I put my cute but tired little elbow on the ELBOW RESTING PLACE,
and in practically no time, it is all
PERKY again!

Would you like to try it? Just put YOUR elbow right on it—the way GROVER did.
THERE! Is that not restful?

Now wait.
I will show you
another
RESTING PLACE.
A

AHA!
I have found another one.
Are you ready to try it ?

An **EAR RESTING PLACE**-
one of my all-time favorites.

This is a FOREHEAD RESTING PLACE.
Go ahead, put your forehead right on it.
"SING"

And this is a THUMB RESTING PLACE! If your thumb is exhausted, let it take a little nappy-poo right here.
AUNT POLLY
Is THAT not comfy?
KARATE INSTRUCTOR

You will simply
ADORE
this next
RESTING PLACE.
"SING

I will give you a hint what it is . . . if you have been smelling a lot lately, this RESTING PLACE is to rest your SMELLER on!
I
LAWNK
PATE

A NOSE RESTING PLACE!
Put your tired old nose on this resting place and in no time you will be smelling like
NEW!

I have many more resting places.
This teeny-weeny little one is a
BELLYBUTTON
RESTING PLACE.
Just put your bellybutton over the
bellybutton resting place.
Make sure you are lined up exactly
right and . . .
GO FOR IT!

WO! I thought it would be easy holding up a teensy little bellybutton RESTING PLACE while you rested your bellybutton on it. I forgot that anyplace you rest your bellybutton, you also rest your belly.
WHEW! I AM PRACTICALLY SQUISHED

HOLD ON.
There are a lot more resting places in here.
The trouble is, there are also a lot of other things in here....
HOME ADORABLE HOME

HOME
ADORABLE
HOME

I had better be careful... or I will make a mess.

This is a CHIN
RESTING PLACE.
A sure cure for a droopy chin.

Put your chinny-chin-chin right there to give it a rest.
It is all right if you have a beard.

Oh, LOOK! Here are my HAND RESTING PLACES.
This is a left-hand resting place.

And this is a right-hand resting place.
BE MY GUEST.

I still haven't found
the best resting place of all.
I **KNOW** *it is in here.*

DON'T GO AWAY.
I want you to see it.

HERE IT IS!
The VERY special, particular
RESTING PLACE
I have been looking for!

A GROVER RESTING PLACE, see? It just fits. I, Grover, am now resting on it as comfy as can be.
TO GROVER with love

In fact, I think I will go to sleep right here and not wake up until tomorrow morning.
If YOU have a resting place, why do you not do the same ?

HOME
ADORABLE
HOME
To GROVER with love
C